For Mum and Dad (J/G),
with all my love x – SK

To the old man, from Miss Mouse!
Thanks for the genes! – ST

SIMON AND SCHUSTER
First published in Great Britain in 2009 by Simon and Schuster UK Ltd
1st Floor, 222 Gray's Inn Road, London WC1X 8HB
A CBS Company
Text copyright © 2009 Sarah KilBride
Illustrations copyright © 2009 Sophie Tilley
Concept © 2009 Simon and Schuster UK
The right of Sarah KilBride and Sophie Tilley to be identified
as the author and illustrator of this work has been asserted by them
in accordance with the Copyright, Designs and Patents Act, 1988
All rights reserved, including the right of reproduction in whole or in part in any form
A CIP catalogue record for this book is available from the British Library upon request
ISBN: 978 1 84738 532 1
Printed in China
7 9 10 8 6

Silver

the Magic Snow Pony

Princess Evie's Ponies

Silver the Magic Snow Pony

Sarah KilBride

Illustrated by Sophie Tilley

SIMON AND SCHUSTER

London New York Sydney

What a busy morning at Starlight Stables! Princess Evie had been busy mucking out her ponies' stalls with the help of her kitten Sparkles. "That was hard work!" sighed Evie. "Now it's time for an adventure. Who's coming today?"

You see, Evie's ponies weren't just any old ponies. They were magic ponies! Whenever Evie rode them, she was whisked away on a magical adventure in a faraway land.

Silver neighed and shook her long mane.

"OK, Silver," smiled Evie. "It's you!" Silver was a small pony

with a soft white coat like fallen snow.

"Come on, Sparkles!" called Evie. But Sparkles wouldn't jump up.

"What's wrong?" she asked. Then Evie realised.

She had forgotten her rucksack full of useful things!

Quickly, she scooped up the rucksack and Sparkles.

Silver cantered towards the
tunnel of trees. Evie closed her eyes.
Where would the tunnel take them today?

Princess Evie gasped as she opened her eyes to a wonderful snow covered world. Now she was wearing a fluffy pink cloak, woolly mittens and snug boots.

Silver's mane and tail sparkled with icicles, and swirling patterns of frost glittered on her bridle and saddle.

As they plodded through the snow, they met two little snow fairies pulling a VERY big sleigh!

"Where are you going with such a big sleigh?" asked Evie.
"We're going ice-skating on Lake Perla," said the snow fairies.
"Do you want to come?"

"Oooh, yes please," replied Evie, excitedly.
"I love skating. My pony, Silver,
is really strong. She can pull your
sleigh if you like."

Soon they were all gliding towards Lake Perla.

Snuggled up in the back of the sleigh, Evie and the
snow fairies sang jolly songs as snowflakes floated
down and landed on their noses.

Suddenly, without warning, Silver stopped.

"What is it, Silver?" asked Evie.

"Look!" cried the snow fairies, pointing. There, at the
bottom of a huge snowdrift, was a tiny polar bear cub.

He looked at them with big sad eyes.

"I've lost my mummy and daddy," he quivered.

"Please help me!"

The snow fairies knew that the polar bears lived in the North and Evie knew that, with Silver pulling the sleigh, they could get the little cub home before dark and still get to Lake Perla in time for skating. There was just one problem — which way was north?

Sparkles had an idea!

He padded over to the rucksack full of useful things

and found a shoelace, a pencil and a compass.

"Well done, Sparkles," cheered Evie.

They all watched the hand of the compass spin

and then point northwards. Off they sped.

As the snow got thicker and thicker, Evie and the snow fairies pulled up their warm hoods. Sparkles and the little polar bear cub huddled up. But soon the snow was flying all around them and Silver couldn't see through it.

They were lost in a blizzard!

"I want my mummy!" sobbed the little cub.

"Don't worry," said Evie. "We'll find her somehow."

But even Evie was feeling a little scared, stuck in the snow.

Just then, there was a loud roaring noise.

"HELP!" cried Evie and the snow fairies together.

But there was no need to worry.

"Momma!" squealed the bear cub and he leapt out of the sleigh, right into the arms of his mummy. "We've been searching for you everywhere," said Mummy Bear and she gave her baby a big hug.

"Thank you for rescuing our little baby,"
said Daddy Bear. "How can we ever repay you?"

"Well," said Evie. "Perhaps you could tell us how to get to Lake Perla?"

"We can do better than that," smiled Daddy Bear.

"Come on, bears. All together!"

The bears helped pull the sleigh out of the blizzard.

Then they gathered around and began humming. The sound echoed
through the air and their icy breath spiralled up to the sky. Princess
Evie looked up to see a swirl of snowflakes above the sleigh.

The flakes whirled and whizzed around them. As they whirled faster and faster, they lifted Silver and the sleigh up into the air. "We're flying!" cried Evie and the snow fairies as they climbed higher and higher into the air. "Bye-bye, bears and thank you!"

They flew over deep snowdrifts and herds of reindeer scraping at the snow. They looked down and saw snow foxes playing together.

Before they could catch their breath, the sleigh landed gently on the banks of Lake Perla. "That was amazing!" gasped Princess Evie. Everyone cheered when the sleigh arrived and soon the frozen lake was full of snow fairies practising their ice dances.

"Come on, Evie!" giggled the snow fairies. Evie put on her ice skates and glided onto the ice. Music floated softly across the frozen lake and all the fairies clapped and sang.

After their dances, Princess Evie and the snow fairies warmed
up with delicious cups of hot chocolate.

Then it was time for Evie, Sparkles and Silver to go home.
Princess Evie gave the snow fairies big hugs.
"Thank you for a wonderful adventure," she said.
"Don't forget to come back soon," smiled the snow fairies.

Off Silver cantered, back through
the snow to the tunnel of trees. Evie turned
and waved to the two little snow fairies.

Back at Starlight Stables, Princess Evie brushed out Silver's mane. Something fell and landed on the ground with a tinkle.

It was a little jewelled purse. Inside, there were two little snowflake hair clips.

"Thank you, snow fairies," smiled Princess Evie. "And thank you, Silver. You're a VERY special snow pony!"

"Miaow!" agreed Sparkles.

Also available:

Star the Magic Sand Pony
Neptune the Magic Sea Pony
Willow the Magic Forest Pony

Coming soon:

Shimmer the Magic Ice Pony